I See Winter

by Charles Ghigna

illustrated by Ag Jatkowska

PICTURE WINDOW BOOKS
a capstone imprint

I see snowflakes passing by.

I see gray geese in the sky.

I see shadows on the hill.

I see frost upon the sill.

I see boots and hats brand new.

I see mittens red and blue.

I see sleds and pairs of skates.

I see icy figure eights.

I see snowmen in a row.

I see angels in the snow.

I see trees without their leaves.

I see smoke rings ride the breeze.

I see cookies on a plate.

I see Grandma decorate.

I see cocoa in a cup.

I see Grandpa sip it up.

I see people in a choir.

I see stockings by the fire.

I see lights upon the tree.

I see a present wrapped for me!

The End

—for Charlotte and Christopher

I See is published by Picture Window Books
A Capstone Imprint
1710 Roe Crest Drive
North Mankato, Minnesota 56003
www.capstonepub.com

Library of Congress Cataloging-in-Publication Data
Ghigna, Charles.
  I see winter / by Charles Ghigna ; illustrated by Ag Jatkowska.
    p. cm.
Summary: Illustrations and easy-to-read, rhyming text show what makes
winter special, from snowflakes and sleds to cocoa and Christmas.
ISBN 978-1-4048-6588-4 (library binding)
ISBN 978-1-4048-6850-2 (pbk.)
 [1. Stories in rhyme. 2. Winter—Fiction.] I. Jatkowska, Ag, ill. II. Title.
 PZ8.3.G345Iaw 2011

 [E]—dc22   2010050089

Creative Director: Heather Kindseth
Designer: Emily Harris

Printed in the United States of America in North Mankato, Minnesota.
122011
006506R